Ruth

Andy Shane

and the
Queen of Egypt

Andy Shane

and the
Queen of Egypt

Jennifer Richard Jacobson

illustrated by Abby Carter

SCHOLASTIC INC.
New York Toronto London Auckland Sydney
Mexico City New Delhi Hong Kong Buenos Aires

For my Uncle Bob—Let me entertain you
J. R. J.

To Carter and Samantha
A. C.

ISBN-13: 978-0-545-15772-8
ISBN-10: 0-545-15772-2

Text copyright © 2008 by Jennifer Richard Jacobson. Illustrations copyright © 2008 by Abby Carter. All rights reserved. Published by Scholastic Inc., 557 Broadway, New York, NY 10012, by arrangement with Candlewick Press. SCHOLASTIC and associated logos are trademarks and/or registered trademarks of Scholastic Inc.

17 16 15 14   18 19/0

Printed in the U.S.A.   40

First Scholastic printing, April 2009

This book was typeset in Vendome.
The illustrations were done in black pencil and black watercolor wash.

CONTENTS

1
I Am the Queen

Andy Shane parked his bike and
shifted the weight in his backpack.
"Let's meet by the *tree* when the
clock says *three*," he said.

"I will ride my *bike*, or we will have to *hike*," said Granny Webb.

Granny and Andy had been talking in rhymes all morning. It was hard to stop once you got started.

"Oh, wait!" said Granny.

"Don't be *late*," said Andy, waving

good-bye.

"No, really," called Granny Webb.

"I have something for you."

Andy turned back to see what
Granny was pulling from her pocket.
Whatever it was appeared to be on
the end of a long gold chain.

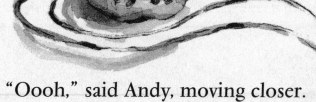

"Oooh," said Andy, moving closer.
It was a dark green bug frozen in
clear plastic. "A beetle!"

"A scarab beetle!" said Granny.

"Is this Egyptian?" asked Andy.

Andy knew that the scarab beetle was important to the people of ancient Egypt.

"I think so," said Granny Webb, handing it to Andy. "I knew you were thinking about African countries last night, and a memory of it popped into my *head* while I was heading off to *bed*!"

Andy laughed at Granny's rhyme. "Thanks," he said, and *he* headed into school.

"What do you think of my new sandals, Andy Shane?" asked Dolores Starbuckle as they sat down at their desks.

"Cool," said Andy.

"I made them myself with milk cartons and glitter," said Dolores.

Andy noticed that Dolores Starbuckle was particularly fancy this morning.

"I hope each of you has chosen an African country," said Ms. Janice. "We need to get ready for the school Culture Fair."

Dolores Starbuckle sat up as tall as she could.

"Polly," said Ms. Janice with her pen in the air, ready to write, "what country would you like to learn about?"

"Kenya," said Polly. "My uncle went to Kenya."

Kenya was a large country with deserts and rain forests. Andy had *almost* chosen Kenya.

"Ahmed?" asked Ms. Janice.

"The Gambia."

Ms. Janice told the class that The Gambia was a small farming country. Andy thought he might like to be a farmer one day.

"Andy Shane?"

Andy touched his pocket. "Egypt," he said softly.

"I'm sorry, Andy," said Ms. Janice. "I didn't hear you."

"I think he said Ethiopia," said Dolores. She was always trying to be helpful.

"Is that right, Andy?" asked Ms. Janice.

Andy shook his head.

"Do you mean Nigeria, Andy Shane?" said Dolores. "I think you mean Ni-*geeeeee*-ria."

"Egypt," Andy said more loudly.

"But you can't choose Egypt," said
Dolores, springing out of her seat.
"I'm wearing my white Egyptian
clothes and my gold jewelry. I even
made sandals. I am the QUEEN
of Egypt."

The class laughed.

Andy slumped down on his desk.

Why did Dolores Starbuckle always

insist on getting what *she* wanted?

But he couldn't argue with her—

not in front of the whole class!

Andy knew everyone was waiting for his answer. He wished he could disappear altogether.

"We'll work this out later," said Ms. Janice. She finished calling on the children. Then she told the class to line up for a visit to the library, where they could begin their research. "Andy Shane," she said, "you're line leader."

Dolores stood in front of Andy.

"Andy Shane, you know I *loooove* Egypt!" she said. "I even have a model of a sphinx!"

"What's a sphinx?" asked Polly.

"A statue. Mine has a lion's body with a bird's head," said Dolores.

"Weird," said Polly.

"But I have this," said Andy.

He pulled out the beetle.

"Oooh," said Dolores, admiring

the necklace. She sighed a long, deep

sigh. Then her face brightened. "Can

we work together, Andy Shane?"

Andy didn't know what to say. He liked to take his time with ideas, see how they felt. And right now, he did not feel like giving Dolores her way. "I'll think about it," he said.

2

Pineapple Pyramids

That night, like every Tuesday night
when her father and mother went to
choir practice, Dolores ate dinner
with Andy Shane and Granny Webb.

Andy was on the kitchen floor coloring a picture of a sphinx when Dolores arrived.

"I wish I could draw like you," said Dolores.

Andy looked up to say thanks, but Dolores was already busy tying on her favorite Granny Webb apron—the one with the big pockets. She hopped up on the stool near the counter.

Granny Webb was emptying chunks of pineapple from a can into a bowl.

"I'll do that, Granny Webb," said

Dolores. "I like to be helpful."

Granny Webb smiled and handed

Dolores the can.

"Wow!" said Dolores. "I never noticed that before."

Andy wanted to say, "Noticed what?" But Dolores went right on talking.

"May I serve the pineapple pizza tonight? *Please?*" asked Dolores.

"Well, it's Andy's turn to set the table, but I'm sure he wouldn't mind some help. Isn't that right, Andy?"

"Sure," said Andy.

After Granny took the pizza from

the oven and let it cool, Dolores

carefully arranged slices on each plate.

Then she stood back and admired

her work.

"My, my, my," said Granny Webb.

Andy came over to see what the fuss

was about. "What *is* this?" he asked.

"Why, Andy," said Granny, "it's pineapple pizza. One of your favorites."

"But how come the pineapple is all piled up on the side of the plate?" asked Andy.

"Don't you see?" said Dolores. "The pineapple chunks are little bricks. I made you a pineapple pyramid!"

"But how come the pizza has bald spots?" said Andy, pointing to his plate. "The pizza and the pineapple are supposed to be together!"

"Think about it, Andy Shane," said Dolores. "The most popular booths at the Culture Fair always have food samples. If we work together on the project, I can make lots and lots of pineapple pyramids! We'll be a huge hit!"

"Oh, brother," said Andy.

Andy knew that Dolores was looking at him while he ate, hoping he'd cave in and say they could work together. But the only thing that caved in that night was his pineapple pyramid.

3

Walk Like an Egyptian

When Andy walked into his classroom the next day, he noticed two things. Number one, Ms. Janice's big yellow bag with orange flowers on it was not beside her desk.

And number two, in the center of Ms.

Janice's desk was a giant stack of paper.

This could mean only one thing.

Andy Shane looked at Dolores.

Dolores Starbuckle nodded.

They were having a substitute

teacher.

Sure enough, a tall man came into the room, explained that Ms. Janice was not feeling well, and handed out work sheets.

Andy finished all the math problems on the page. Then he began drawing pictures of baseballs and baseball bats all around the edge of his paper. According to Andy Shane, today was the best day of the year. It was the first day of T-ball!

Dolores cleared her throat.

Andy looked up to see what she was doing.

She was writing their names in Egyptian hieroglyphs.

Andy pretended he didn't see.

The tall man handed out a second set of work sheets, and then a third. When Dolores had finished her third paper, she asked the substitute teacher if they could make get-well cards for Ms. Janice.

"A wonderful suggestion!" said the

substitute.

Andy Shane reached into his desk

to find his crayons. He pulled out his

action figure of Giraffe Man.

"Hey!" he cried. His Giraffe Man

was wrapped up in toilet paper.

"Doesn't he make a

great mummy?" asked Dolores.

"Ugh!" said Andy. After he finished

his card, he would draw a sign for his

desk that read *No Trespassing.*

That evening, Andy's coach asked
Andy to play right field. In T-ball,
you have to have a strong arm to
play right field.

Andy Shane looked at the bleachers
to locate Granny Webb. Sitting next
to Granny was Dolores Starbuckle.
Andy Shane couldn't help noticing
that she was *still* wearing her
fancy Egyptian clothes.

Both teams had batters that had
no trouble hitting the ball off the tee.
By the final inning, the score was
tied. A girl known as Slugger was up
next. Andy adjusted his cap and
backed up. He would be ready.

Suddenly, music blared from the
stands. Dolores was standing on
the top bleacher. Only she wasn't just
standing. She was dancing. She was
dancing to a song called "Walk Like
an Egyptian."

Andy knew that Dolores loved this song. She loved showing others how she could walk like an Egyptian along with the music. She strutted and turned, strutted and turned.

People in the stands applauded.

But Slugger wasn't watching
Dolores. She got into position,
pulled back the bat, and popped
that ball into right field.

"Catch it, Andy!" yelled Granny Webb.

But Andy didn't catch it. He was too busy watching Dolores. So were the other kids in the outfield.

The ball rolled past Andy and hit
the back fence.

Slugger scored a home run, and her team won the game.

Andy Shane would not even look at Dolores when he came off the field.

At that moment, she was not the queen of anything.

4

A Team

That night Andy couldn't get to sleep.

First, he couldn't believe he had

missed the ball and lost the game.

Second, he knew that tomorrow he had to stand up and tell the class his plans for the Culture Fair. Whenever Andy had to speak to the whole class, he felt as if his throat took a dive and hid somewhere deep in his stomach.

"Here's a 'sorry' note," said Dolores as Andy walked through the classroom door. It was in Egyptian hieroglyphs.

"Do you want me to read it to you?" asked Dolores.

"No," Andy said. He didn't even
try to read it. He just stuffed it into
his pocket.

Later, when the class was painting an enormous map of the continent of Africa, Dolores handed Andy the paintbrush with the blue handle. Everyone in Ms. Janice's class knew that the brush with the blue handle was the biggest and the best of all.

"No, thanks," said Andy. He didn't even look at Dolores when he spoke.

When the painting was finished, Ms. Janice asked each student to come to the front of the room and give a report on his or her Culture Day plans.

Peter went first. He showed the class pictures of masks from Mali. "I'm going to make a mask," he said.

Polly showed the class a mobile
she was working on. Hanging from
the mobile were pictures of the desert,
the forest, the seashore, and a big
city. All of these places were in
Kenya.

"Andy, show us what you've done," said Ms. Janice.

Andy walked to the front of the room. He began to speak but realized he had nothing in his hands. Peter had shown something. Polly had shown something. What should he do?

"I want—" Andy paused. "I want . . ."

"Your mummy!" said Dolores.

Everyone laughed.

Dolores reached into Andy's desk and took out Giraffe Man. She handed him to Andy.

"Oooh," the students said.

Andy Shane held the mummy action figure but still looked as if he didn't know what to say.

Dolores waved her hands from the

back of the room to get

his attention.

She made

her hands go

around her neck,

like a necklace.

"I have a necklace," said Andy, "that

has a scarab beetle on it. People in

ancient Egypt believed that the scarab-

beetle god pushed the sun across the

sky. And . . ."

"Yes, Andy?" said Ms. Janice.

Dolores made her hands and face look like the sphinx that Andy had drawn at home.

"Oh, I made a picture of a sphinx," said Andy.

"You should see Andy's picture, Ms. Janice," said Dolores. "It came out really well!"

Andy could feel his face getting warmer, but he was happy. He took a big breath and sat down.

"Thank you, Andy," said Ms. Janice. "Dolores, why don't you come up and tell us about the country you've chosen."

Dolores walked to the front of the room.

She pointed to the map the children

had painted and said, "I've chosen the

teeny tiny country of Togo, which is—"

"No!" shouted Andy.

All eyes turned to him.

"Andy?" said Ms. Janice.

Andy stood up. "Dolores and I are going to work together—on Egypt."

"Really?" asked Dolores.

Andy nodded.

"Oh, thank you, thank you, thank you, Andy Shane!"

For a minute, Andy was afraid Dolores was going to hug him. Or she was going to strut back and forth doing her Egyptian dance. Instead,

she simply wiggled her toes in her

Egyptian sandals and smiled.

rful," said Ms. Janice.

smiled back. There was no

abt about it. He and Dolores

Starbuckle, the Queen of Egypt,

would make a great team.